Lollipops

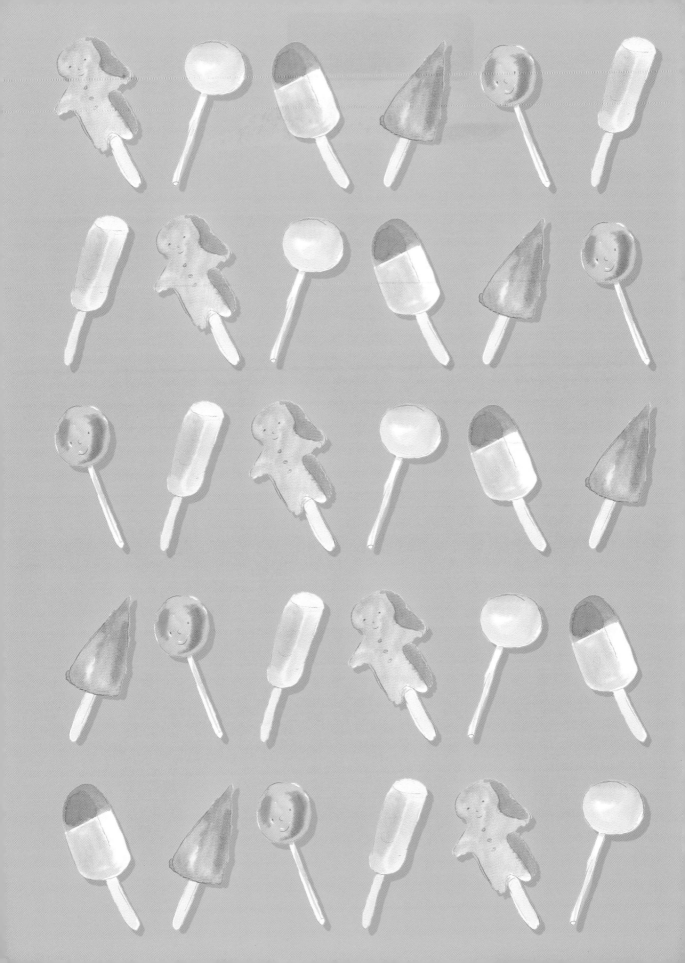

Bare Bear

and other rhymes for
young children

Original Poems by **John Foster**

Illustrated by **John Wallace**

OXFORD
UNIVERSITY PRESS

Oxford University Press, Great Clarendon Street, Oxford OX2 6DP

Oxford New York
Athens Auckland Bangkok Bogotá Buenos Aires Calcutta
Cape Town Chennai Dar es Salaam Delhi Florence Hong Kong Istanbul
Karachi Kuala Lumpur Madrid Melbourne Mexico City Mumbai
Nairobi Paris São Paulo Singapore Taipei Tokyo Toronto Warsaw

and associated companies in
Berlin Ibadan

Oxford is a trade mark of Oxford University Press

Text copyright © John Foster 1999
Illustrations copyright © John Wallace 1999

The author and artist have asserted their moral right to be
known as the author and artist of the work.

First published 1999

British Library Cataloguing in Publication Data
Data available

ISBN 0 19 276207 9

Printed in Hong Kong

Contents

Bare Bear

Bare Bear has no hair.
Where? Oh, where
Is Bare Bear's hair?

Jenny found the scissors.
Snip! Snip! Snip!
Jenny found the scissors.
Clip! Clip! Clip!

'It'll grow again,' Jenny said.
But her mother shook her head.
'I'm afraid not. Oh dear, no.
Teddy bears' hair doesn't grow.'

Bare Bear has no hair.
Where? Oh, where
Is Bare Bear's hair?

There! There!
Under the chair!

Crocodile one, alligator two

Crocodile one, alligator two
Who's been causing a hullabaloo?

Elephant three, rhinoceros four
Who's been banging on the kitchen door?

Monkey five, chimpanzee six
Who's been getting up to lots of tricks?

Penguin seven, walrus eight
Who's been swinging on the garden gate?

Kangaroo nine, donkey ten
Who's been getting up to mischief again?

Letters

One, two, three, four—
Posting letters
Through our door.
Who's got a letter?
Who are they for?

One's for Ali.
One's for Sue.
One's for me
And one's for you!

Jaspar Jolly

Jaspar Jolly sat on some holly.
He jumped in the air with a shriek.
Though he bandaged his bottom
Where the holly had got him,
He couldn't sit down for a week.

Rosemary Rudd

Rosemary Rudd
Says, 'I like mud!'

It's squelchy! It's gooey!
It's sticky! It's gluey!

You can pick it up and hold it.
You can shape it. You can mould it.

It slips and it slops.
It drips and it drops.

It gets between your fingers.
It gets between your toes.
It gets itself all over you—
It gets right up your nose!

It gets on your ears.
It gets in your hair.
But Rosemary Rudd says,
'I don't care.'

Rosemary Rudd
Says, 'I like mud.'

Bouncing, bouncing

Bouncing here, bouncing there,
Bouncing, bouncing everywhere.

Bounce on your bottom, bounce on your feet,
Bounce down the garden, bounce up the street.

Bouncing here, bouncing there,
Bouncing, bouncing everywhere.

Bounce to the playground, bounce to the school,
Bounce to the park and the swimming pool.

Bouncing here, bouncing there,
Bouncing, bouncing everywhere.

Bounce to the car park, bounce to the car,
Bounce, bounce, bounce wherever you are!

Scuttle like a crab

Scuttle like a crab.
Creep like a snail.
Swim like a dolphin.
Dive like a whale.

Stalk like a lion.
Pounce like a cat.
Jump like a kangaroo.
Run like a rat.

Wriggle like a worm.
Hop like a frog.
Wag your tail
And pant like a dog!

The Band

Listen to the rhythm!
Listen to the beat!
Here comes the band
Marching down the street.

Hear the trumpets tooting.
Hear the cymbals clang.
Hear the big drum booming.
Bang! Bang! Bang!

Hear the rat-a-tat.
Hear the drums beat.
Hear the tramp, tramp
Of the marching feet.

See the baton twirl!
See it thrown up high!
Hear the people cheer
As the band goes by.

My clockwork rabbit

My clockwork rabbit hop, hop, hops.
Then he runs down and stop . . . stop . . . stops.
I carefully wind him up and then
He hop, hop, hop, hop, hops again.

My big cardboard box

My big cardboard box is a tall sailing ship
That skims across the foam.
I load it with treasure from pirate wrecks
Before I head for home.

My big cardboard box is a silver rocket
That takes me to the stars.
I race through space to set up a base
And explore the surface of Mars.

My big cardboard box is a huge aeroplane.
I fly to golden sands,
Where lollipop trees and ice-cream flowers
Grow in a magic land.

There's nothing like a cardboard box
To take you far away,
When you're stuck inside with nothing to do
On a wet and windy day.

I like to hear

I like to hear the telephone ringing.
I don't like to hear my sister singing.

I like to hear sausages sizzling.
I don't like to hear the baby grizzling.

I like to hear dinosaurs roaring.
I don't like to hear my dad snoring.

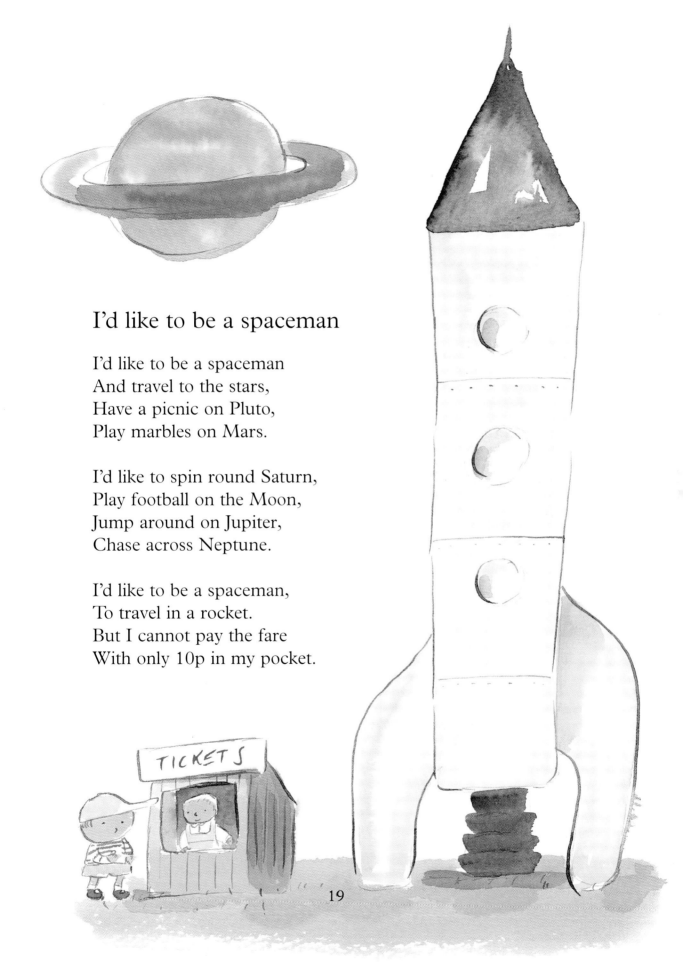

I'd like to be a spaceman

I'd like to be a spaceman
And travel to the stars,
Have a picnic on Pluto,
Play marbles on Mars.

I'd like to spin round Saturn,
Play football on the Moon,
Jump around on Jupiter,
Chase across Neptune.

I'd like to be a spaceman,
To travel in a rocket.
But I cannot pay the fare
With only 10p in my pocket.

TICKETS

Skip down the path

Skip down the path.
Hide in the shed.
Race round the roses.
Stand on your head.

Roll in the grass.
Swing on the swing.
Jump in the air.
Dive through the ring.

Slide down the slide.
Chase round the tree.
Run out of breath.
Go in for tea!

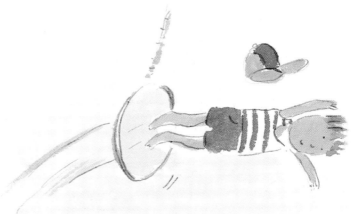

Oh dear, it's raining

Oh dear, it's raining.
We can't go out to play.
We could finish the jigsaw
We started yesterday.

Don't want to finish the jigsaw.
Want to go out to play.

Oh dear, it's raining.
What would you like to do?
We could play hide-and-seek.
I could hunt for you.

Don't want to play hide-and-seek.
Don't want to play with you.

Oh dear, it's raining.
Do you want to read a book?
Do you want to bake some cakes?
Would you like to cook?

Want to go out in the garden.
Don't want to read or cook.

Look! It's stopping raining.
The clouds have blown away.
We can go out in the garden.
We can go out to play.

Let's go out in the garden!
Let's go out to play!

Tastes

Jelly's slippery.
Ice-cream's cold.
Toffee's sweet
And sticky to hold.

Curry is hot
And full of spice.
Crisps are crunchy.
Chocolate's nice.

Chinese, please

Chinese, please!
Chinese, please!
We want Chinese for our teas.
Oodles of noodles,
Chicken and rice,
We think Chinese meals are nice.

Chinese, please!
Chinese, please!
We want Chinese for our teas.
Beef chop suey,
Chicken chow mein,
Please can we have Chinese again?

Washing up

My older sister says
That washing up's a chore.
But I like washing up.
I don't think that it's a bore.

Splish, splosh,
Splosh, splish.
Swirl the water round each dish.

Splosh, splash,
Splash, splosh.
Give the frying pan a wash.

Splash, splish,
Splish, splash.
The plates are clean, in a flash.

My older sister says
That washing up's a chore.
But I think washing up is fun!
Can I do some more?

There's a dragon in the sky

There's a dragon in the sky
Watch it dive and swoop!
See it shake its snaky tail
As it loops the loop.

There's a dragon in the sky.
I painted it bright red.
I made it with my grandpa
In his garden shed.

There's a dragon in the sky,
Dancing, flying free.
There's a dragon in the sky
And it belongs to me.

I'm not scared of the monster

I'm not scared of the monster
That hides beneath my bed.
When it leaps out
To prowl about,
I pat it on the head.

I'm not scared of the monster
That lurks behind the door.
When it leaps out
To prowl about,
I shake its furry paw.

I'm not scared of the monster
That skulks under the chair.
When it leaps out
To prowl about,
I stroke its spiky hair.

I'm not scared of the monsters,
'Cause they're no longer there.
When I leapt out
To scream and shout,
I gave them all a scare!

Dinosaur dream

Dinah Shore dreamed she saw
A dinosaur peeping round her bedroom door.

Dinah Shore dreamed she saw
A dinosaur knock on her window with its claw.

Dinah Shore dreamed she saw
A dinosaur sleeping on the kitchen floor.

Dinah Shore dreamed she saw
A dinosaur wake up and give a mighty ROAR!

Wizard Bear

If you trap your fingers in the door,
Or fall and bang your knee on the floor,
Who's always there to cuddle and care?
Wizard Bear.

If you hear a noise during the night,
Have a bad dream and wake with a fright,
Who's always there to cuddle and care?
Wizard Bear.

If you're full of cold, lying in bed,
With a runny nose and aching head,
Who's always there to cuddle and care?
Wizard Bear.

If you're down in the dumps, feeling sad,
If you've done something naughty and bad,
Who's always there to cuddle and care?
Wizard Bear.

Night-time

The sun has slipped behind the hill.
The flowers' petals are closed and still.
The birds in the trees are silent now
As they softly settle upon the bough.
In his basket the dog breathes deep,
Puts head on his paws and falls asleep.

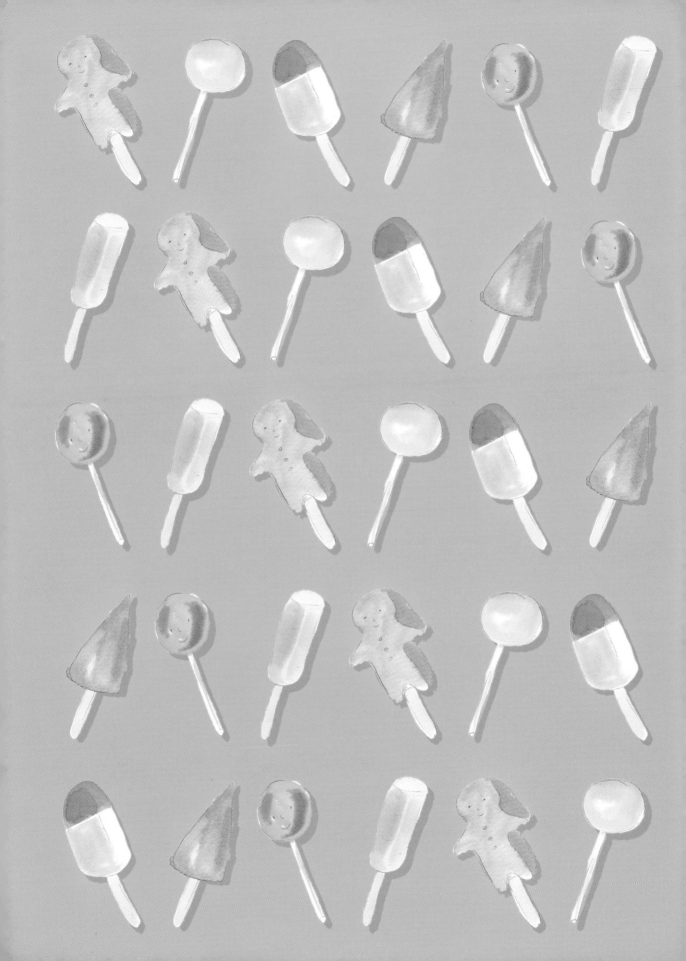

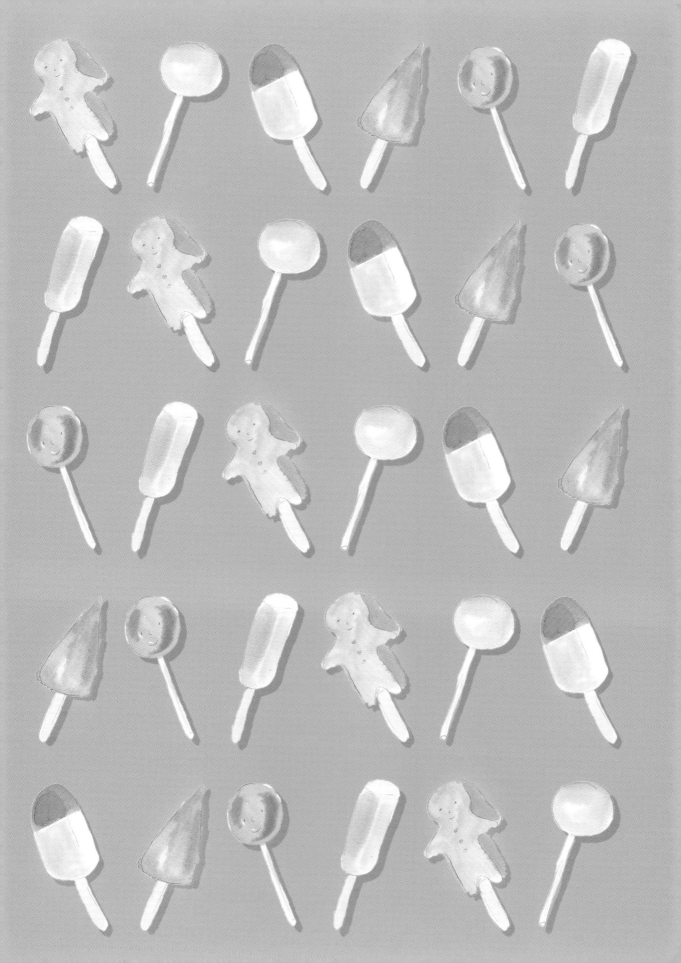